MYSTERY SHORT STORY COLLECTION VOLUME 4

CONNOR WHITELEY

No part of this book may be reproduced in any form or by any electronic or mechanical means. Including information storage, and retrieval systems, without written permission from the author except for the use of brief quotations in a book review.

This book is NOT legal, professional, medical, financial or any type of official advice.

Any questions about the book, rights licensing, or to contact the author, please email connorwhiteley@connorwhiteley.net

Copyright © 2024 CONNOR WHITELEY

All rights reserved.

DEDICATION
Thank you to all my readers without you I couldn't do what I love.

A THERAPY WAY TO GO

Retired Detective Kendra O'Connor had always enjoyed the amazing work of therapists, and they had seriously helped her more times than she cared to admit after the loss of friends, partners and witnesses that she had failed to protect. Thankfully, all those losses were still in the single figures but over the decades they certainly added up to a heavy burden.

Thankfully there were amazing therapists to help people through these difficult times.

Yet Kendra had to admit as she went into the beautifully decorated conservatory with floor-to-ceiling windows forming the walls and thick wooden beams forming the stunning roof and a few pillars for support, she couldn't deny private therapy spaces were certainly getting more cosy since she had last been to therapy.

She really liked the therapy space's white tile floors that had a hint of gold running through them to make them feel less clinical. There was a large coffee table made from walnut wood and it was just such a great little feature.

Kendra had always loved her own coffee table at home with her husband but she had never considered how a simple brown coffee table could add such texture and depth to a room. She hated how her husband might be right about her watching too many interior design programmes.

Kendra just smiled to herself as the weird hints of bleach, dust and damp filled her senses, leaving the strange taste of stupidly dry chicken on her tongue like how her mother used to cook. Her mother seriously couldn't cook to save her life.

A gentle autumn breeze blew through the conservatory and Kendra was glad it wasn't too cold nor too warm. It was just right for a day of investigating and at least there were two large neutral-coloured sofas for her to sit on.

They looked rather new and very maintained but Kendra just knew the therapist murder victim was a great woman that only wanted to help make her clients feel as comfortable as possible.

Mrs Helen Carter was a 50-year-old psychotherapist that had worked in the NHS most of her life before her parents died and left her and her husband a ton of money. Then Helen set up her own private practice and she was thriving by providing people affordable psychological care.

She had helped a ton of people over the past decade but one night the husband had popped out to get a takeaway and when he came home Helen was dead. There were no traces of a murder so it was ruled a suicide until two weeks ago when someone called the police with "new evidence". The police never found the caller so the case went cold again.

It was amazing cases like these that made Kendra proud to be a member of the Cold Case Task force dedicated to solving London's most twisted, impossible and evil cold cases.

Kendra really wanted to solve this one but her best friends still hadn't turned up.

"My driving was fine,"

Kendra laughed as she saw her two best friends in the entire world come into the conservatory. Retired Officer Patricia Nelson looked as beautiful as always in some black trousers, a white blouse and a very nice rose gold necklace that somehow managed to take ten years off her.

And Kendra was so glad to see she had her black laptop bag like always. She still had no idea how 70-year-old something Patricia had better computer skills than her grandchildren, but at least it meant Kendra didn't have to use the damn things.

Then Kendra smiled at Retired Detective Jeff Long who looked as smart as always with his long black business suit. He might have certainly looked his age but Kendra still loved him as a friend, but she couldn't understand the slight tension between them.

"What's wrong?" Kendra asked.

Pataricia just smiled. "You know there's road

work on the hill where we live taking us onto the motorway. Well this smartass decided *he* would drive us here using country roads. And let me tell you my car isn't built for country roads and it seriously isn't built for driving across fields in the interest of shortcuts, Hun,"

Jeff laughed. "Maybe that wasn't my finest moment,"

Kendra just shook her head. Even after all these years she still couldn't understand how Pat and Jeff could get into weird adventures, but they were amazing together and she would always treasure them. They really were something special.

"You both read the case file?" Kendra asked.

"Of course Hun," Pat said, "and has anything been touched since the murder?"

"No," Kendra said, "not a single thing has been moved since the murder three years ago. Even the husband doesn't really come in here even on really nice days,"

"That's awful," Jeff said. "I can't find anything the original detectives did wrong on the case. It looked like suicide if you take out the husband,"

"Why was the husband taken out?" Kendra asked knowing it wasn't clear from the case files.

"Hun, there was no evidence tying anyone to the crime and the GPS in his car and the CCTV footage in the takeaway shop checked out. They both show he wasn't at the house at the time of the murder,"

Kendra nodded. It made sense because out of

everything she had read about the marriage, it seemed perfect or maybe a little too perfect.

"Have you got the CCTV footage?" Kendra asked Pat.

Pat nodded as she sat down on the sofa and turned on her laptop resting it on the coffee table. Kendra watched as Pat pulled up the footage and Kendra had to admit it looked exactly like the husband.

"Run this footage through one of your programmes please to see if it's been faked or something," Kendra said.

Pat just laughed and Kendra smiled too. She always liked having a friend with access to illegal computer programmes that a mere citizen really shouldn't have had.

"Confirmed, everything checks out. This is the husband at the takeaway at the time of the murder, Hun,"

Kendra rolled her eyes and looked at Jeff who was inspecting the other sofa as that was where the body was found.

Kendra went over to him and from what she remembered in the case file the body was found with a single stab wound to the chest and then the body was positioned like she was sleeping on the sofa.

It certainly wasn't a normal position for a victim to be in and Kendra couldn't help but realise that the killer believed they had time to focus on the presentation of the body. She had seen a lot of killers in her active career and even more as a Retired Detective but this made no sense.

How would the killer know they would have time to position the body?

"Hey," Kendra said, "what if the killer wasn't only watching the house but they had help as well to keep the husband away?"

Jeff shook his head. "Damn it,"

"Actually Hun that theory might be correct," Pat said. "I checked the roads, phone logs for the takeaway the night of the murder and I checked the surrounding area for any crime reports,"

"Did you find something?" Jeff asked.

"Yes Hun, the phone logs were a bust and the traffic was perfectly okay but the husband would have been delayed by five minutes. There was a 999 caller of a wife beater in the area and the description matched the husband perfectly,"

"Only delayed by five minutes? I presume the police caught the husband and checked his story," Jeff said.

Kendra nodded. She was surprised the cops didn't just arrest him under caution just to be on the safe side.

Kendra paced round the conservatory a few times.

"Maybe Hun that's what the killer wanted but police records show the officers released the husband because he was able to confirm he didn't live at the address the police officers wanted and they did not believe him to be a wife beater,"

"At least they were right about that," Kendra said.

Kendra was surprised the killer would go to so much trouble just to make sure the husband wasn't home. The killer had to be extremely clever, evil and such a foul person to want to do all of this.

"What about her clients?" Jeff asked.

"All checked out," Kendra said. "She mainly helped people who don't meet NHS requirements, so basically anyone who isn't suicidal. She mainly treated people with relationship difficulties, trauma and abuse,"

Kendra coughed a little as she got a massive whiff of the horrible bleach and dust combination. It was such a horrible smell but that wonderful cool breeze was really nice.

"The clients all had alibis too Hun,"

"What about," Kendra said looking at Jeff, "this was done by a rejected client? What if someone came to Helen for help and she rejected them for some reason? Maybe she didn't have the knowledge to help them, maybe she was too full and maybe she was just too busy,"

"That's a good point," Jeff said, "I don't remember seeing a rejection list in the case file,"

"That's because the original cops didn't take it Hun," Pat said, "but I know Helen backed up everything online and she actually kept a folder of rejected clients in case this happened and in case her schedule was freed up so she could contact them,"

"How many names?" Kendra asked.

"Way too many,"

Kendra went over and she forced her mouth not to drop at the sheer sight of all the rejected people. She knew there was a mental health crisis going on but this was unreal and extreme. She had no idea this many people felt the need to go private because they just wanted to improve their lives but there was no other way for them to get help.

"I'll cross-reference the names of these clients with the police databases and my own special programmes to see if something pops up," Pat said.

"Do we want to know where these programmes came from?" Jeff asked.

Kendra just shook her head. "Probably not but that's why we're retired. A lot less rules and paperwork and the legality of putting the case together can be left to the active detectives within reason,"

"I love retirement," Jeff said laughing.

"So do I," Kendra said as she went over to the conservatory doors. They weren't anything that special and rather annoyingly she didn't think they would be that hard to simply force open, but from what she had read about Helen she always left the doors open for a while after a client had left.

Even more so on a beautiful evening with a delightfully cool, refreshing breeze. Kendra could seriously relate to that.

"Got something Huns," Pat said.

Kendra went over to her friend and smiled as she realised there were only two suspects on the list. One was a man had requested mental health support with his relationships and trauma and abuse that stemmed from his childhood.

He had popped up in the search because he had recently posted a good number of hateful posts about how his life was stupid, he needed to die and he hated the entire world.

Kendra really hoped he could now get NHS mental health support because he was clearly at breaking point.

Then the other person was a woman who wanted support dealing with her grief and loss difficulties, because she had lost friends, family members and other important people in traumatic and shocking ways. Kendra couldn't believe how devastating some of these events were as she read the woman's notes.

But Kendra just shook her head as she looked at the reason why the woman had been flagged. Pat didn't seem to notice but Kendra recognised some of the searches the woman had made. She was looking for ways to kill someone, get revenge and eventually commit suicide.

She wanted something painless and quick.

Kendra gently took Pat's laptop and searched if the woman was still alive and thankfully she was. She was currently in a high-security institution for suicidal individuals and there was a note attached to the police record, something about an assault on staff members two weeks ago when she had placed an unknown call.

"What do you want to bet that was the call to the police about the suicide not being a suicide?" Kendra asked.

Jeff shook his head. "I'll contact the active detectives and get them involved,"

***

Two days later, Kendra was flat out loving sitting out on the cool black rattan garden suite her and her husband had bought a few years ago. She loved how stylish, cool and great it looked in their tiny little garden, that was nothing more than a small square with some flowers, grass and a patio area in it. The advantages of living in a tiny terrace house in the middle of central London.

The flowers might have been starting to turn brown and dry up and die as the season turned, but she didn't mind. Kendra was looking forward to the seasons turning because it meant the start of another time of her life and autumn meant the cases would only get weirder, more complex and cold at their very heart.

Something that seriously kept her enjoying life as a retired detective. It gave her life purpose, hope and meaning besides from being a wife, mother and grandmother. They were all great things too but she loved her job.

The delightful cool evening breeze made Kendra smile more and more and she could understand why

Helen had enjoyed the evenings so much. So maybe it was good in a way that she died in the evening and breeze she loved.

Kendra was so excited about the sensational dinner of garlic, chicken and mint her husband had cooking away. She loved those incredible flavours and even now the taste of that dinner was thankfully forming on her tongue. She couldn't wait.

It was even better when Kendra had gotten a phone call from Jeff explaining how the active detectives had arrested and gotten a full confession from the woman, who had confessed to the killing because she was so angry at the world for continuing to take away her nearest and dearest. It had taken her years to gather up the courage to get professional help and she was in so much pain, so when Helen said no. It killed her inside and she continued to spiral.

She had tried to reach out to other places but they rejected her too so she got a number of awful ideas in her head about how she needed to kill herself but also punish others at the same time.

All leading to her plotting and killing Helen Carter. The therapist that could have saved her but decided not to.

Kendra just watched her beautiful husband as he got up to finish off their sensational dinner and she couldn't deny that she loved her life. She felt sorry and awful for what so many other people were going through, and she knew how much pain mental health could cause.

But there was always hope, there was always a reason to live and there was always reason to find joy. Kendra knew it might have been hard to find it at times but it was always there.

And it was always wonderful to find in the end and if a person needed it Kendra always encouraged them to take up therapy. It was a great way to go.

THE WAR PROFITEER
1ˢᵗ November 2022

London, England

Now normally in the cool and hardly mild month of November I, hitwoman Anna Robinson, like to start my Christmas shopping a little early, I start preparing for my charity fun runs and I start visiting my children that are living all over the world at this point, and I truly love all of them.

But right now I was sitting on top of an icy cold grey metal rooftop on top of a massive warehouse building that stretched on for hundreds of metres and was good twenty metres tall.

The sky was very overcast, dark and it looked like it was about to rain at any moment, and thankfully I had dressed in my correct "killing" uniform because of it. which today was a long waterproof trench coat, jeans and trainers that meant I could run as fast as I wanted without being restricted.

I had a little gas stove next to me boiling some

water for me at the moment and the light sound of boiling water and the slight roar of the gas burner filled the air. Along with sounds of workers smoking, lorries driving below and in the distance the city of London was starting to wake up today.

The disgusting aromas of cigar and cigarette smoke mixed in the small amounts of lorry exhaust filled the air, and I hated the smell. I had never liked it when my dad smoked them when I was a kid and I hated it even more now.

This wasn't exactly how I intended to spend my morning but when I was hired to kill someone.

I killed them.

Below me was a massive concrete road filled with a few green shipping containers, three small groups of black uniformed workers smoking and there were tons of lorries constantly moving and driving past.

This area on the outskirts of London was part of some new local government strategy to increase the UK productivity, so of course it wouldn't work, but it was nice that they were trying and I was far more interested in my target that was bound to show up today.

Neta Oakwood was the very worst type of human on the entire world in my opinion, because she was a war profiteer and now she was a millionaire after supplying arms and weapons and tanks to the UK, Russia and Middle Eastern terror groups.

Of course, MI5 and 6 and a bunch of other international security agencies had tried to kill her for one and tried to get evidence of her corruption for a prosecution but they had failed completely.

So the heads of MI5, 6 and the French Directorate-General of External Security had hired me to assassinate her and they thankfully had already paid me in full.

Now I just hate war profiteers because I am no saint or pacifier, I like a good war as much as the next person, it was why I served in the Royal Marines for two years before I got fired for enjoying the killing too much. So now I kill people for about ten times as much as I made in an entire year in the Royal Marines, I did love my job.

And apparently the damn war profiteer was meant to be arriving here today because a shipment of missiles were coming and she wanted to inspect them personally.

All the workers below me stopped talking and quickly stomped out their cigars and cigarettes when a group of three black SUVs pulled up. The men in black suits got out of the front and back car first looked around and clapped their hands together for ten seconds straight.

And yes that really did look as weird as it sounds.

A very tall and elegant woman was the only person to step out of the middle SUV and she did look good. She was wearing black trousers, a blue blouse and a very thick and extremely expensive white fur coat that was probably real fur. Yet another reason to kill her.

My only rules in life are family first, don't kill innocents and don't kill animals. Clearly this damn war profiteer didn't care about innocent lives in the slightest.

As my little gas stove made the water boil more and more, I turned it off and grabbed my black rucksack behind me. I always carried it with me but I rarely look at it until the target arrives.

I took out my collapsible rifle from my rucksack and I started aiming at her.

Some of the workers hugged her and kissed her hand and then they all stopped and froze instantly.

I was about to shoot the woman dead when I saw another much larger black SUV roll out and even Neta seemed annoyed that the SUV was here.

The SUV stopped and a very overweight middle-aged man got out but he somehow managed to make the weight work on him.

"You shouldn't be here Toby," Neta said.

That name was strange because it sounded so familiar and it was even stranger that the man looked even more familiar like I had actually met him. He certainly wasn't involved in the files and casework that I had been sent by the intelligence agencies for the hit.

He looked so familiar though.

"I will go wherever I please to get my weapons for my Government," Toby said.

It was only now I was realising that these two were shouting at each other across a good ten metres and not one of them seemed interested in getting closer to the other.

"The UAE will get their missiles sooner than they expected," Neta said starting to turn away.

Toby took a few steps closer. All the men that had stepped out of the SUVs with Neta whipped out pistols.

This wasn't good for me at all. These men with Neta were highly trained and were very armed and probably wouldn't give two thoughts about killing me, or at least swarming the warehouse and cutting off my escape.

I had dealt with so-called impossible odds before but even I had my limits.

The sound of lorries driving on the other side of the warehouse made me smile because there was a tiny chance if I could run the tens upon tens of metres to the other side of the warehouse. I could hopefully jump off the warehouse and land on a lorry all before the SUV men caught me.

But I was depending on a lot of ifs with that plan. The biggest one being that a lorry would be approaching the warehouse when I needed it to.

"Calm down Toby," Neta said as I saw two of her men hold Toby's arms and effectively restrain him.

Then I immediately realised where the hell I had seen him before, he was an international arms-dealer that always acted as a broker for arms deals between hostile governments and dealers.

I couldn't understand why the UAE wanted western missiles but that didn't matter to me, it was above my pay grade and I would sell that little detail to MI6 and donate the money to charity.

And I really can be that nice at times.

I noticed six more SUVs turn up and Neta's face dropped.

"You didn't think I wouldn't bring UAE special forces with me?" Toby said.

Damn. This was really getting out of hand now because each of those SUVs contained at least five special forces operatives and it would only take one of them to kill me.

I had to carry out the hit now and escape.

I aimed my sniper rifle but I didn't actually know who to kill exactly.

Sure I was meant to kill Neta because she was the target of my contract and it was my duty to my clients to kill her. But this Toby man was also a war profiteer that made money by giving hostile governments evil weapons to use against innocent people.

Who was more important? The supplier of the weapons or the person who gave the weapons to the killers?

Fuck it. I had to kill both of them and just hope that their security details didn't get too much of a lead on me whilst I killed the other.

And hopefully I would start a firefight between the two groups because I was hoping that the other group would believe I was hired by the other side to kill the other.

I aimed my rifle.

I shot Neta in-between the eyes.

Everyone screamed. Panicked.

The two groups shot at each other.

I aimed my rifle at Toby.

I shot him *in* the eye.

I jumped up.

Someone tackled me to the ground.

A woman started punching me. Again and again.

She wrapped her hands round my throat.

I grabbed my gas stove.

Crippling pain filled my hand.

I swung the gas stove.

Boiling water splashed over the woman.

She screamed in agony.

I jumped up.

And kicked her off the building.

I looked down at the fighting below. Tons of people were missing.

Bullets slammed into the metal around me.

I looked at the side of the warehouse that had the metal staircase I had used to get up here in the first place.

Men were climbing up there.

I picked up my gas stove again.

I charged.

I had to get to the other side of the warehouse roof.

More bullets smashed into the floor around me.

I threw the gas stove.

I shot at it.

The gas stove exploded.

Some of the men caught on fire.

I kept running.

Two men tried to tackle me to the ground.

I leapt over them.

I kept running.

I got to the end of the warehouse.

There were three lorries driving past.

I ran backwards.

I ran forward.

I jumped.

Landing on the head lorry in the group.

Twenty men charged out at the end of the road making the lorry stop.

I couldn't fucking ass around anymore.

I ran across the lorry roof.

Climbed down the side of the driver's compartment.

I smashed open the driver's door.

Pulled the driver out.

And I simply climbed inside the lorry.

I slammed my foot on the accelerator, I ran over tons of men and I made my escape.

***

It turned out in the end MI6 bought my little shard of information about the UAE for a mere ten thousand pounds. I don't really know why I was in such a generous mood but I just was. I really enjoyed working with them and now a homeless charity had that ten thousand pounds and I was okay with it.

Of course over the next two hours after I had escaped, all the men in their SUVs had chased me, climbed up on my lorry and tried to kill me but I killed them all.

And after so many people climbing up on the canvas roof of the lorry, it had collapsed trapping over thirty men inside.

So I did the responsible thing and drove the lorry into a freezing cold lake and I watched all the men drown. And if any managed to escape the lorry then I shot them in-between the eyes as they were swimming. It was a lot of fun actually and I was seriously looking forward to working with MI6 and the other intelligence agencies again.

I was still sitting on the cool leaf-covered ground by the massive lake as I made sure that no more bodies were going to pop up and I was perfectly warm in amongst the trees and just enjoying the sheer beauty of nature.

Because at the end of the day, I really did only care about making sure innocent people and animals were safe and didn't die, it was the guilty that suffered and the world was a better place because of my actions.

And today the world really was a better place because I had killed a war profiteer, assassinated an arms-broker and I had helped to starve hostile governments of killing machines. And that seriously was a good day's work to me.

And I could certainly sleep better tonight.

FUTURE BAKING

Cheaters will always exist in competitions regardless of whatever the future promises.

The sweet, beautiful aromas of sweet honey boiling away gently on a hob, sweet vanilla cakes cooking slowly in the oven and the gentle rolling boil of homemade jam filled the large white canvas tent that Celebrity Chef Janet Hart was standing in near the front.

This was the first-ever finals of the Great Kent Cook Off and she absolutely couldn't believe that she was finally here, finally getting to judge a cooking show, just like her mother had wanted before she had sadly died of cancer a decade ago.

Janet had to admit that even after ten episodes and ten weekends with all the amazing amateur bakers, the entire setup and tent was still brand-new to her and she was constantly struggling to find where everything was, but she seriously loved this job.

She still enjoyed watching the bakers and cookers chop, slice and mix ingredients like they were babies as they stood behind their tall wooden counter with bright copper ovens (their sponsor's choice, not

Janet's) and they were all wearing the custom-made aprons made by yet another sponsor.

The tent was covered in so many blues, reds and whites that she sometimes felt like she was walking into the Union Jack every weekend, but as soon as her co-presenter shouted *Cook* she was in her element.

It was incredible seeing what some bakers were up to these days and trying to combine different combinations of ingredients that Janet had never had the pleasure of eating.

There were three contestants in the final today and Janet was so impressed with them all. Rachel was a typical grandmother baker with long grey hair, pink jumper and she focused on old recipes. Janet wasn't sure if she was going to win but she seemed to be doing enough to impress her and her co-judge.

Robert was another good contestant with his attractive poufy black hair and slim body, who managed amazing flavours every single day but he definitely lacked presentation skills at times. He would never get a job at her restaurants but he was a great guy to be around.

And Sarah was probably the best of all of them if only she could keep her head in the game just long enough to win. Janet admired how driven, strong-willed and bold Sarah was and it almost always paid off but Janet really hoped that she wouldn't make a mistake that would cost her everything.

In fact, Janet was worried about that herself.

Ever since she was a little child she had been watching, studying, learning from cooking shows as much as she could and it was so surreal actually being a judge of her own one but she hated it when her phone buzzed.

Janet took out her brand-new holo-phone that her grandkids had bought her and she managed to unlock the little thing.

And she really hadn't wanted to get an alert from the tent's security equipment showing her that nanobots were present in the tent.

She had never wanted to get the security equipment but the Streaming service had insisted on it with the other claims of cheating on the other cooking programmes and viewers were starting to abandon cooking programmes because of all the cheaters.

Janet understood that, but on her programme she was focusing on how cooking used to be done back in the 2010s and 2020s before the technology of nanobots, robots and all the other methods of cheating got created.

Baking wasn't an art anymore.

A person could simply programme nanobots to create a cake, add them to water and place the water in a hot oven and ten minutes later a person would have a cake that tasted amazing.

That wasn't baking, but hell it was what everyone else was doing. It was why everyone at the streaming service had jumped on Janet's idea for an old-fashioned baking competition.

That was all in doubt now.

Janet looked around for her co-judge and she was laughing in front of the camera after explaining how something worked in baking.

Janet really did love Josephine. She was a smart presenter, very camera friendly and the UK loved her so Janet had no problem asking her for help launching the programme.

And considering that Josephine had been busted with a lot of younger escorts a few months back, she needed to get her career back on track and since it was just an innocent situation made to look bad, Janet was perfectly okay to help out a friend.

It was the least she could do.

As soon as the camera people took their little floating orbs away, Janet went over to her and turned her back to the bakers.

"We have a problem," Janet said, "security system has found nanobots in the tent. I cannot say where they are or who's using them but we have a problem,"

Josephine weakly smiled pointing to the fact that her mic was still on.

Damn it. Janet hadn't even realised that their mics were on all the time during a challenge so the streaming service instantly knew there was a chance cheating was going on.

For the sake of the programme, their future and their careers, Janet had to find out who was using the nanobots and deal with it quietly before this became a national scandal.

And the idea of home, old-fashioned baking was well and truly killed forever.

Janet covered her mic. "How do we find these nanobots? Do they come in a packet or something?"

Josephine shook her head also covering her mic. "I used those nanobots once and they come in a small glass tube with a computer adapter on the end so you can programme them,"

Janet nodded. She didn't care that Josephine had used them before, part of being a good cook was being able to experiment and get creative.

Janet wiped a drop of sweat off her forehead as the temperature of the tent rose more and more. The challenge they had set the cookers was the very last one of the entire series.

The cookers had to create three different complex desserts and the challenge was about to end in fifteen minutes. That was all the time they had to discover who was using the nanobots.

"So we're looking for someone having a glass tube in their bin?" Janet asked.

Josephine gave a camerawoman a fake smile as she passed and shook her head. "I don't know but I doubt it. We could carefully search the bins but what if the criminal has the tube on them?"

Janet shook her head and walked towards the bakers, pretending to be inspecting them decorating their cakes and everything, when she was actually wondering who the hell would risk their reputation and hers over something as stupid as nanobots.

After the past weekends with them, she considered all of them friends so it was just outrageous that they would betray her trust like this.

Janet went over to Robert who was working on making fondant icing for his massive, very-light chocolate mousse cake. It wasn't exactly as fancy or complex as Janet would have liked but it did look impressive, despite it being out of the fridge when it seriously should have been in one.

Maybe he was the user of the nanobots and that was why he wasn't putting the cake in the fridge. Maybe he was a cheater.

Janet shook her head and kept walking around the tent, she managed to look at Robert's bin as she paced but it was empty, completely empty, it was a little weird but not uncommon. The production crew were amazing at their job.

This production crew were far better than she ever was when she was working behind the scenes a few years ago.

Janet went over to the camera people who were crowding around Rachel because she was making spun sugar by making some caramel, flicking it in the air and then the caramel created very thin threads.

It was probably the most advanced thing she had ever tried but she looked like it was going to be placed on top of a Victoria Sponge. Definitely not complex and unless her other two desserts were stunning, there was no chance of her winning.

Janet really wanted to help Rachel by recommending some advanced techniques to at least give her a fighting chance, Rachel was kind and loved her family but Janet couldn't help her.

Hell, even a homemade crème diplomat would help her a great deal and it wasn't even that hard.

As Janet watched the camera people focus their camera orbs on Rachel's "good" side, she just couldn't help but wonder if Rachel was using nanobots to help herself win.

Actually, there was a fairly good chance considering that Rachel worked as a technology engineer during the week, working on massive projects all over England.

Janet frowned as Rachel had said repeatedly how she hated nanobots because they destroyed the art of baking, cooking and creating bread. Janet was sure she was right but that also meant she couldn't be the user.

Unless that had all been an act.

Janet wanted to stomp her feet on the ground. She was a chef, she wasn't a sleuth and she had no idea how to begin to properly investigate this potential crime.

"Five minutes left!" a very tall woman shouted, one of the streaming service's top presenters.

Janet was about to go over to Sarah when she realised that the top presenter actually hated her because the presenter had thought she was some hot-shot baker but Janet had confessed the presenter's biscuits were far worse than her three-year-old grandson's burnt offering the other week.

And that was definitely the truth.

Janet just watched the presenter, called Megan, as she offered words of encouragement, jokes and more to the three remaining bakers and she just knew that Megan was the type of person to sabotage someone's career.

There had been rumours of it for years and Janet had always dismissed them as jealous rumours by people who didn't get the job. Maybe they were right.

"Camera people over here please," Megan said grinning. "I have an announcement and a confession to make,"

Janet looked at Josephine who was studying Sarah's technique for a moment and their eyes locked.

Stop her. Josephine mouthed.

Janet nodded as she quickly picked up Rachel's piping hot mug of tea and she speed-walked over to the camera people.

She kept walking. Getting faster and faster.

She pretended to trip.

Janet threw the boiling hot mug of tea all over

Megan just before the camera crew started filming.

They all laughed at Megan and they turned off their camera orbs for a moment as Megan started swearing.

Janet folded her arms and everyone just stopped in the tent as Josephine also came over.

"You know this show is a fraud. All these bakers are using nanobots. I'll destroy you all," Megan said.

Janet shook her head. "You forget dear Megan, the crew have stopped filming, your mic is destroyed and of course the streaming service has all our audio data. They will destroy it and you used the nanobots anyway,"

Megan spat at Janet. "You righteous cow. I am the best baker in the UK and I'll prove it to you,"

Janet couldn't help but laugh at the poor silly woman as Megan shook her fist harder and harder in Janet's direction.

"You will never do anything in TV again because there is no proof of the nanobots and everyone in the tent except me signed an NDA so you can never talk about it. And I certainly will not,"

"Security," Josephine said as two women stormed in and dragged Megan from the set.

Janet turned towards the contestants and they were all actually done. They hadn't abused the distraction and used the extra time to finish off their creations, they had simply stuck to the rules like professional bakers and cookers.

And that made Janet damn proud of all of them.

"Places everyone," a man shouted from the camera crew. "We need to film the ending,"

Janet just laughed because showbusiness never ended and she was so excited about tasting all these delightful creations with her favourite co-judge at her side.

***

The next few hours had been just amazing, Janet was really impressed with how Rachel had created some perfectly executed classics just like how Janet's mother used to make. Including a perfectly done Victoria Sponge, Sticky Toffee Pudding and a sensationally sweet and fruit jam tart, but it just wasn't that creative.

Janet was also seriously impressed with Robert because his flavours were just incredible and she had no idea before now that chocolate, coffee and some strange spice from India she had no idea how to pronounce actually worked. All of his desserts were immense explosions of flavour on the tongue, but it was just a shame that his souffle had dropped just a centimetre.

That just wasn't good enough for Janet. Of course Josephine had tried to convince her that one single centimetre was being too strict and without nanobots it was impossible to stop a souffle from falling, but Janet had managed without it.

It had hardly been a surprise to her and Josephine that Sarah had won by creating three professional-level French desserts that deserved to be in a top-level patisserie and Janet wasn't even sure she could manage some of those crisp, sweet, stunning desserts but no one needed to know that for sure.

So after all the chaos of the past few weeks, the cheating and Megan getting blacklisted from the TV industry forever, Janet was so looking forward to going back to her own cafes and restaurants and kitchens so she could do what she absolutely loved.

She loved baking and cooking and creating brand-new things to add such joy to people's lives that she knew she was never going to give it up. And she was looking forward to the next season of her programme because she realised now she wasn't just a judge on some random cooking show, she was actually protecting the future of baking by making people want to do it once more.

And that was truly a great thing to protect. Something she would happily do until the day she died.

THE EVENT INVOLVING THE STORE, THE GUN AND THE MAN

Retired Social Worker Judy Allen was so relieved as she sat in her little black Ford Aztec with its wonderfully soft fabric chairs, cold dashboard and the cool conditioned air blowing out towards her face. Judy had never liked really hot days like this one, she never had and she doubted she ever would but at least she was finally in the underground parking lot.

She wasn't exactly sure why it was so empty, considering it was the size of two football pitches with bright white lights illuminating every nook and cranny. Judy really wanted the store to do something with the cold grey concrete walls, but she knew they wouldn't.

Judy would have loved to paint them, maybe stick up some posters or just do something else with them entirely. The cold greyness of it all just made her feel so damn depressed, lonely and she wanted to go towards the store entrance more than anything. At least she would be with other people that way and not in the cold darkness of the lot.

Judy leant over to her left and got a massive whiff of her vanilla-scented air fresher that her beautiful husband had got her last week. She really did love how he was always getting her little gifts, presents and surprises. It was great to feel loved after so many bad relationships in the past.

The sweet vanilla aroma was even better when the great taste of vanilla ice cream formed on her tongue. She really did need to kidnap the grandchildren again and take them to the beach. As far as Judy was concerned all beaches had the best ice cream and she had definitely tested that fact over the years.

Judy popped open her glovebox and grabbed her purse, a Bag for Life and a small phone that she had been meaning to return, she had simply never gotten round to it. The soup kitchen, the trauma support group and all her other little hobbies had kept her busy.

Judy got out the little Ford and she smiled as she shivered. The underground air-conditioning was amazing, brilliant and it was such a wonderful contrast to the sheer heat of outside. It was always moments like this that made Judy realise she seriously needed a new car, one that had good air-conditioning but the car got her from A to B so there was no point.

No point at all.

Judy couldn't understand the strange scent of petrol in the air. There were no other cars in the parking lot and there was no one else. The sheer silence of the parking lot was confusing as hell, it was rather maddening actually.

Judy started walking over to the grey metal door on the other side of the parking lot. It was a small set of stairs that would take her to the store and Judy was really not looking forward to the aroma of wee that always filled that staircase.

Her footsteps echoed in the sheer silence and Judy couldn't understand what the hell was happening. It was a Saturday morning and there were always people here, normally in the hundreds.

But there was nothing today.

All the parking spots with their thick white lines were still there. They weren't covered up by bad drivers or anything.

She was still thrilled that she had managed to get a parking spot without crashing or hitting anything this time. That was so bad when she had hit a small concrete block on the way in and destroyed her bumper.

She was fucking mortified that a young couple had been watching her. Even now she hated parking lots because of it. It was flat out the worst thing she had ever experienced.

Judy shook the foul memory away and she opened the cool metal door and almost gagged at the strong smell of urine that overwhelmed her senses. It was just so damn disgusting that people pissed in the stairwell, it was just wrong on every single level.

Judy covered her mouth and nose with her little hand and she managed to focus on the chipped concrete steps in front of her. They all curved to the right and there was a rusty metal handrail with blue paint cracking off of it.

She went up the stairs and she was glad she could start to hear voices. They weren't the normal volume of happy children, shouting parents and teenagers singing for one reason or another. But it was still better than the weird silence of the parking lot.

And Judy couldn't deny the smell was getting a lot better too. The staircase now smelt like she was walking *past* a toilet instead of walking through it.

The large blue fire door was up ahead with a small window and Judy grinned as she opened it. She was finally going to be able to start her shopping, she needed to return the phone and then she wanted to buy something for her husband.

A little treat would be great.

Judy went through the door and the amazingly sweet aromas of vanilla, cake and rich buttery pastries filled her scents as the store had a brand-new bakery section and café.

It looked great and Judy was almost surprised this store had done something so classy, modern and fresh. The huge sterile white counter stretched for tens of metres with glass cabinets on top. Judy so badly wanted to go over and look at all the professional-grade cakes, pastries and other delights hiding under the glass but ultimately urging her towards them.

She had to get the shopping done first.

The temptation was even worse when Judy saw Stephanie in her little white apron pop up from behind the counter. Her long black hair looked so carefully styled today, she was grinning like always and her normal look of blue jeans and a white blouse under the apron suited her even more today. Judy had been meaning to see Steph for ages now because she was going back to university soon and it would have been great to catch up before then. Judy really had to slow down for a while and focus on her friends instead of all her charity stuff.

She was going to have to talk to Steph later on over a great big mug of coffee.

She loved the bakery even more as her mouth got excited as the brilliant tastes of strawberry shortcake, iced buns and Victoria Sponge formed on her tongue. She was so going to have to check it out later on.

Judy was about to peel herself away from the bakery when she noticed that yet again, all the sterile white little round tables of the café were empty. There were small menus, sauces and even free samples on each of the tables, all designed to be elegant and enticing.

Yet Judy could only focus on one man that she hadn't noticed a moment ago. He was sitting alone and wearing a black tracksuit, horrible black trainers and there was a large bag of something next to him. It looked like a black messenger bag but she wasn't sure.

And as much as Judy just wanted to go and crack on with her shopping, she really had a bad feeling about him. She could see that Stephanie was looking at him, clearly scared and that young woman wasn't scared of anything so Judy had to deal with him.

Judy went over to him and he looked up immediately. Judy couldn't deny he wasn't a bad-looking man at all, his blue eyes were soft, calm and gentle but his evil smile spoke volumes.

"I would leave if I was you," the man said. "I'm going to start killing in a moment,"

"Where is everyone else?" Judy asked really hoping the man hadn't killed anyone yet.

"I don't know to be honest," the man said, "hopefully away from here because your friend Steph has called her boss and when he turns up I am going to kill him,"

Judy had no idea how the hell she was going to stop this but she just had to. Steph was clearly too scared and she was too young to die in some vain attempt to save her boss.

Judy had to stop this man and she was going to have to channel her former Social Worker skills in order to get through to him.

"Steph," Judy said, "can I have a large mug of coffee please? A flat white,"

The man just looked at Judy as she pulled out a

chair. The plastic was a little cool against her fingers but Judy just wanted to save lives here even if she didn't know Steph's boss.

"Why do you want to kill him?" Judy asked noticing the man was moving his hand towards his bag.

"Why does it matter who I kill or not?"

"I'm actually more interested in why the police hadn't been called. I know there aren't a lot of people here but come to think of it, it was the World Cup final last night and I presume we did well. A lot of people are probably hungover,"

"And who goes shopping at 8 a.m. on a Saturday morning?"

"True," Judy said, at least she now knew the man had thought about this extremely carefully.

Judy smiled at Steph as she came over and she really liked the sterile white mug that Steph placed in front of her with a small caramelised biscuit on the side. This place had really gone up market.

"I presume Steph's boss must be involved in something criminal for him not to want to call the cops.

Steph coughed and Judy nodded as that was all she needed.

"Clearly it isn't uncommon knowledge about his business dealings," Judy said. "How much is he stealing and why do you care?"

The man leant forward. "Because that boss man killed my brother in a way. He charges *protection* against himself on the store owners and it's stupidly expensive,"

Judy nodded. "Let me guess if they don't pay up then they have to get out of the mall and then the problems get worse,"

"He snapped by brother's fingers and then when he closed down my brother's store, my brother had to declare bankruptcy,"

Judy gasped and took a sip of her wonderful flat white. She loved the slight bitterness that filled her mouth that was perfectly accented with the creaminess of the milk and slight sugar.

"I'm sorry that happened,"

"Then there was his suicide after his wife took his kids and divorced him,"

"God," Judy said taking another wonderful sip of the coffee.

"You see I have to kill him. I have to make him suffer and I have to-"

Judy waved him silent. "No you don't because there are other ways and there are ways for you to get justice for your brother. You can expose him, surely?"

"No," the man said. "I tried all of that over the past two weeks. I went to the police every single day, I went to Financial Conduct Authority every single day, I wrote to my MP every single day. No one cares about this criminal activity and no one cares about my brother,"

"I care," Judy said.

She just looked at the man's relief, fear and

desperation in his kind eyes and she just knew he wasn't lying. After so many decades as a social worker hearing about the worst of humanity, she had a good instinct for when someone was lying to her.

He wasn't.

"Steph," Judy said gesturing her to come over.

"What?" she asked standing about a metre away from Judy.

"What happened to your store and how much does he charge you for protection?" Judy asked.

The man pulled a gun out of the bag and Judy really hoped Steph didn't see that. Judy felt her heart pounding in her chest and sheer fear gripped her.

"I don't know. Maybe two thousand a month, it will cripple us soon enough," Steph said. "I know the bakery's mine but my business partner is already to jump ship,"

Judy grinned. She was seriously impressed that Steph had started up the bakery and café herself, maybe she wasn't going back to university soon and maybe she was doing it online or something. Judy really had to find out.

"I thought you were going to uni?" Judy asked.

"I'm doing my final year online so I can focus on my business. It's a degree in Business Management so it makes sense,"

Judy nodded. "Amazing news, I'm really proud of you,"

"Women," the man said. "What about my brother?"

Judy just looked at Steph because there was no easy decision here, no easy way out and no easy way to make sure Steph's business stayed intact. It was clear that a business owner had to go on record and explain about the protection money and all the other criminal things going on here.

But if Steph went on record then Judy knew the bakery and café would be shut by the end of the day, the next few years would be hell with the trial and her boss and owner of the Mall would do everything in his power to destroy the chance of her business ever developing.

What was more important?

So Judy explained all that to her.

"Um," Steph said pacing around.

Judy looked at the man because she could see he wasn't impressed or maybe he was just concerned. This couldn't have been easy for him and she really wanted him to let go of the gun.

"Give me the gun," Judy said quietly.

The man shook his head. "Not until she agrees to go on record. My brother deserves that much,"

"Killing anyone will not help your case. This will only hurt you and make you even less believable to the authorities," Judy said.

The man frowned and after a moment he put the gun back in the bag.

"Thank you," Judy said as she finished off her coffee and smiled as Steph came over.

"I'll do it but I need somewhere else to set up

shop," she said.

"What do you do for a living?" Judy asked the man.

The man grinned. "I'm a high-end property developer that focuses on the commercial side of real estate,"

"And I am sure after threatening my friend and myself with a gun and threatening to kill us too, that you would be happy to give her a discount on a new place?" Judy asked grinning because he seriously didn't have a choice.

"That would be my pleasure," the man said through ground teeth and he shook both their hands.

Judy just looked at Steph. "You never called your boss did you?"

"Nope, but I will now call the police for sure,"

Judy just let out a massive breath she didn't know she was holding and she really hoped justice would be served.

***

A few hours later when Judy got back inside her little black Ford, she was so damn proud of herself, the man that she now knew was called John and Steph for everything they had done today. John had managed to slip away into the night without anyone actually knowing he had technically committed a crime by threatening to hold her and Steph at gunpoint.

Steph had been amazingly brave and she had revealed the extreme extent that her evil boss had threatened her, her business and her store. She had even managed to provide evidence for it all and her boss had been arrested a few minutes ago.

Judy just allowed the wonderful cool fabric of her chair to claim her body as she looked forward to getting home. She had gotten a new phone for one of the grandkids, she had brought her husband some weird gadget that he would love and life really was perfect.

As much as she loved the brilliant vanilla aroma of her car air fresher, she was still a little concerned because the entire park lot was filled to the brim now with tons upon tons of red, blue and white cars of various makes and models. If an accident was going to happen then it would happen now but Judy knew she would be okay.

And even if she wasn't then she had still had a great day where she had helped to expose a criminal, she had gotten justice for a brother and she had had a brilliant day shopping for the people she loved. And Judy was thrilled to be going out with Steph tomorrow for dinner and then to see the brand-new building she was going to buy for her new bakery and café.

It was going to be the perfect end to a perfect weekend. A weekend that Judy was going to treasure forever.

FINDING TRUTH

"Did you expect him to die?"

John Zelly just smiled to himself as he allowed the wonderfully soft white sand to absorb his bare feet as he went on the beautiful beach him and his old best friend Julie were on searching for an old ring. John might not have been there for years but he still loved it more than he wanted to admit.

The beautiful crisp crystal-clear waves were gently lapping onto the beach. John loved how the delightful sound of the waves passing over the fine white sand made everything more intense in a good way, and everything was a lot more relaxed.

He hadn't been to any beach in decades, not since his children had grown up and decided family days out on the beach weren't cool anymore. He had missed the incredibly refreshing, intense salt-scented air, wonderful coolness of the sea and just how the beach helped put everything into perspective.

"John?" Julie asked.

John smiled as he looked at his old best friend, the beautiful woman he had once loved and she still looked stunning in her white dress that was perfectly made for her. It highlighted how her middle-aged body might have been older but it was still majestic.

Julie started gently kicking at the sand and John just rolled his eyes.

"No I didn't want Nathan to die as quickly as he did," John said focusing on the sand himself despite it all bloody looking the same. "Why's this ring important anyway?"

"Because this ring belongs to Nathan's mother and he would want it at the ceremony later,"

John nodded as he could feel her intensely beautiful glaze staring at him. He couldn't have cared less about some dumb ring and Nathan hated his mother anyway so John couldn't understand why Julie wanted to get him alone to talk.

"The ceremony starts soon. Should we, you know, get up there and see what's happening before our other friends turn up?" John asked poking at the sand without any luck finding the damn ring.

John noticed Julie was kneeling on the sand now digging about. John didn't doubt the sand was cool and wonderful against bare skin but he didn't want to get his business suit dirty, Nathan would probably rise from the dead and punish him.

"The ring must be found," Julie said.

John wanted some dark clouds or something to overcome but the damn universe or whatever nonsense the hippies called it weren't playing ball. The stupid sky was perfectly clear and John just wanted to shout at Julie. She was hiding something from him.

"Why? We both know Nathan hated his mother, he hated his childhood and he hated the night we killed his father," John said.

John shook a little as he actually spoke the words aloud for the first time for decades. None of them had ever agreed to talk about it again, none of them had even acknowledged it happened but they were all guilty of murder to various extents.

No one was more guilty than Nathan though.

"You said it. Wow," Julie said standing up and dusting the sand off her dress.

John looked at his first love and smiled. He wanted her to know they were completely alone and whatever they said here was just between them, just like the murder so long ago.

"I wanted to tell so many people about that night. The night we killed another man for no good reason,"

John shrugged. "We were all young kids, scared of what was going to happen and it had all started on a beach just like this one,"

John couldn't blame Julie as she shook a little and went back to gently kicking the sand to try and find the damn ring none of them really cared about. But the ring had to be found so he could at least talk about that night.

The night that had been haunting him for decades.

"It was you, me and Nathan at first on the beach, we were just drinking and talking about our plans for the future," John said smiling. "I loved those times when we could just talk,"

"Definitely," Julie said laughing. "Then Josh, Juliet and Pipper joined us and then two hours later Nathan told us what happened at home,"

John just stopped and he just felt cold, so damn cold despite the warm sun beaming down on them.

"When Nat told me," John said, "about the abuse at home I didn't know what to say,"

"Did any of us?" Julie said kneeling down on the sand again and clawing at it with her bare hands.

"I guess not but we did what we could. We comforted him, allowed him to talk and he told us how his parents hated how he was moving to a new city, he was a failure and he was a foul son of theirs,"

"I don't think his choice of girlfriends helped back then,"

John laughed. "Maybe not but Lisa was a lovely girl. People just couldn't see past the fact that her parents were in prison for dealing drugs,"

"True that," Julie said throwing a peddle into the sea. The deafening splash almost made John jump.

"Then it was simple," John said. "After Nat told us everything we just didn't want him to suffer anymore,"

"Wait a minute we did not go from talking to plotting a murder just like that," Julie said standing up. "Did Nat show us something? Cuts and bruises,"

John gasped. It had taken him years to stop waking up in a fearful sweat at night thinking about the sheer horror of those cuts and bruises all over Nat. It was actually why Nat had quit all the sport teams, they were simply too painful for him.

"That made Josh, Pipper and Juliet angry and that was how the rage started," Julie said.

John went over to her and just looked at her beautiful face. "The rage? I remember it differently I think it was Josh himself that suggested we go and talk to Nat's parents in a big group,"

"But there was rage?"

John shook his head. "No. No there wasn't. Everyone was upset and sad more than anything and concerned for Nat, no one was rageful. Even Josh wasn't and we know the sort of temper he had back at school,"

John went to hold her as she fell back a little and almost went into the sea but she waved him away and recovered before the waves could reach her.

"How have you been all these years?" John asked.

"Well," Julie said laughing. "It takes me a sleeping pill a night to enter a light sleep and another glass of whiskey to sleep through the night. I killed him that night,"

John just hugged her. He could feel her resisting but he didn't care because she was in pain and she was flat out wrong about the events that night.

"You didn't do anything and I think both of us are punishing ourselves for what we only witnessed," John said.

"How have you been all these years?"

John laughed. "Oh my children don't talk to me because I was never emotionally there for them as children. My wife divorced me three years ago because I was too distressed at night and I couldn't talk about this with her,"

"But you did nothing," Julie said smiling.

John was about to bury his face in her neck like how they used to as teenagers for comfort but Julie pushed away. She went back to searching for the damn ring.

"I know Josh was suggesting we go and see him. I don't really remember what happened next until the murder," John said.

"That's easy. Pipper and Juliet agreed with him and they were actively planning what they were going to say. Then you and me were comforting Nat who was really silent, motionless and not himself,"

"That boy really was the life and soul of a party at school, wasn't he?" John asked.

"Yeah. I remember he was my first kiss and wow, that boy could seriously kiss,"

"He could seriously do anything. He could sell mice to elephants, get anyone to agree with him and he could play any sport he wanted to," John said.

"But he couldn't do maths to save his life,"

John laughed. "Oh shit yeah he was so bad at maths. And yet he was great at physics which is half-maths. Amazing kid,"

John smiled as the gentle crashing of waves got a little louder for a moment until it went back to being almost silent. He really did love the beach because it always helped to put things in perspective, the beach was sort of magical that way.

"Then," Julie said finding a small pile of black stones under the sand, "we started going towards Nathan's house because Josh wanted to confront his parents. We went along to make sure nothing bad happened and then we knocked on the front door,"

"It was a great house though," John said, "their front garden was stunning with all those roses, tulips and sweetpea just growing perfectly. My mother would have killed to have a garden like that,"

John smiled as Julie waved him silent.

"We knocked on that horrible wooden front door and Nat's mother was out. The father answered and maybe that's when we should have called this off," Julie said moving the stones and searching under each one.

"Why?" John asked. "I know his father was wearing a massive smoking jacket, he was smiling and he was pleased to see us. He was offering all of us a drink and some dinner if we wanted it,"

"I know and I'm not talking about that aspect. I'm talking about the way Josh had grabbed the father and was shouting and screaming,"

John just shook his head and sank down on his knees into the wonderfully fine, cool sand. He had thought about that rage for so many decades.

He hated that it had happened and Josh was so out of control and Nat, poor Nat was feeling too dead inside to even talk.

"We went inside," John said, "to try and get Josh off the father but... Josh pushed the father and then it happened,"

"I can still hear the crack of his head as he fell and hit one of the steps," Julie said. "The crack of the skull and all the blood that followed,"

"Nat just started crying and he became a corpse himself. You and me had to hold him whilst Josh, Pipper and Juliet cleaned up. They wiped up our fingerprints on the front door and it was the 90s so there were no cameras at home,"

Julie smiled as she lifted up one of the rocks. "And then we ran. No one was home on the little street that night so we all came down to the beach, this very beach and made a pack never to talk about it,"

John went over to her and grinned in a way that made his face hurt after frowning for more decades than he cared to admit. He looked down at the beautiful diamond ring that hadn't belonged to Nathan's mother.

It was Julie's and John remembered now that at the beach that night the pack was bound together by the ring. When the time was right and the ceremony was held, the ring would be brought to it and the truth about that night would be revealed.

And all of them would finally be free of the horrible burden they had been carrying since that awful night.

"You know we couldn't have changed anything right?" John asked.

Julie nodded. "I know that now. For the first time in years I feel like I haven't had a ton of weight on my chest and I now know the truth. I wasn't at fault, I wasn't the killer and I was only a young girl trying to protect me abused friend,"

"Same," John said feeling so much lighter for finally realising it himself. "How did Nathan die?"

Julie just hugged John and John understood. They had all tried in different ways to get Nathan to get professional help over the years but John knew, just knew some people couldn't be helped because they weren't ready.

Nathan never was ready.

"He jumped off a cliff near here actually," Julie said.

John just hugged the beautiful woman even tighter. He didn't even care about cracking one of her ribs, he just needed a hug after all these decades of pain, suffering and trauma.

"He would be proud of us two you know," John said. "He would have liked to know we're still friends, we had their conversation and that we can move forward with our lives together,"

"Together you say?" Julie asked grinning like the beautiful teenage girl she had once been.

John extended his arm. "Come on Julie we didn't

date all those decades ago because of the murder. Why are we still letting the past control us?"

Julie wrapped a wonderfully warm arm around his and John loved the feeling because it was so right, natural and sensational. It was all he had ever wanted since he was a little boy.

And as him and Julie started walking along the delightful fine sandy beach towards the main path back towards the church where the ceremony was being held in private, he was so looking forward to seeing everyone again.

Josh and Pipper and Juliet would all be there and finally they could reveal what they had done to each other, and the truth could be revealed to all. Only because they had found some silly ring, but still a ring that John was glad to have found.

It hadn't only unburdened himself today, helped Julie with her own pain but he had gotten his true love back too. And that was the most precious feeling he had ever had and he would always treasure that until the waves stopped crashing gently against the beach.

MYSTERY SHORT STORY COLLECTION VOLUME 4

GET YOUR FREE SHORT STORY NOW!
And get signed up to Connor Whiteley's newsletter to hear about new gripping books, offers and exciting projects. (You'll never be sent spam)

https://www.subscribepage.io/wintersignup

About the author:

Connor Whiteley is the author of over 60 books in the sci-fi fantasy, nonfiction psychology and books for writer's genre and he is a Human Branding Speaker and Consultant.

He is a passionate warhammer 40,000 reader, psychology student and author.

Who narrates his own audiobooks and he hosts The Psychology World Podcast.

All whilst studying Psychology at the University of Kent, England.

Also, he was a former Explorer Scout where he gave a speech to the Maltese President in August 2018 and he attended Prince Charles' 70th Birthday Party at Buckingham Palace in May 2018.

Plus, he is a self-confessed coffee lover!

Other books by Connor Whiteley:
Bettie English Private Eye Series
A Very Private Woman
The Russian Case
A Very Urgent Matter
A Case Most Personal
Trains, Scots and Private Eyes
The Federation Protects
Cops, Robbers and Private Eyes
Just Ask Bettie English
An Inheritance To Die For
The Death of Graham Adams
Bearing Witness
The Twelve
The Wrong Body
The Assassination Of Bettie English
Wining And Dying
Eight Hours
Uniformed Cabal
A Case Most Christmas

Gay Romance Novellas
Breaking, Nursing, Repairing A Broken Heart
Jacob And Daniel
Fallen For A Lie
Spying And Weddings
Clean Break

Awakening Love
Meeting A Country Man
Loving Prime Minister
Snowed In Love
Never Been Kissed
Love Betrays You

<u>Lord of War Origin Trilogy:</u>
Not Scared Of The Dark
Madness
Burn Them All

<u>The Fireheart Fantasy Series</u>
Heart of Fire
Heart of Lies
Heart of Prophecy
Heart of Bones
Heart of Fate

<u>City of Assassins (Urban Fantasy)</u>
City of Death
City of Martyrs
City of Pleasure
City of Power

MYSTERY SHORT STORY COLLECTION VOLUME 4

<u>Agents of The Emperor</u>
Return of The Ancient Ones
Vigilance
Angels of Fire
Kingmaker
The Eight
The Lost Generation
Hunt
Emperor's Council
Speaker of Treachery
Birth Of The Empire
Terraforma
Spaceguard

<u>The Rising Augusta Fantasy Adventure Series</u>
Rise To Power
Rising Walls
Rising Force
Rising Realm

<u>Lord Of War Trilogy (Agents of The Emperor)</u>
Not Scared Of The Dark
Madness
Burn It All Down

Miscellaneous:
RETURN
FREEDOM
SALVATION
Reflection of Mount Flame
The Masked One
The Great Deer
English Independence

OTHER SHORT STORIES BY CONNOR WHITELEY

Mystery Short Story Collections
Criminally Good Stories Volume 1: 20 Detective Mystery Short Stories
Criminally Good Stories Volume 2: 20 Private Investigator Short Stories
Criminally Good Stories Volume 3: 20 Crime Fiction Short Stories
Criminally Good Stories Volume 4: 20 Science Fiction and Fantasy Mystery Short Stories
Criminally Good Stories Volume 5: 20 Romantic Suspense Short Stories

Mystery Short Stories:
Protecting The Woman She Hated

MYSTERY SHORT STORY COLLECTION VOLUME 4

Finding A Royal Friend
Our Woman In Paris
Corrupt Driving
A Prime Assassination
Jubilee Thief
Jubilee, Terror, Celebrations
Negative Jubilation
Ghostly Jubilation
Killing For Womenkind
A Snowy Death
Miracle Of Death
A Spy In Rome
The 12:30 To St Pancreas
A Country In Trouble
A Smokey Way To Go
A Spicy Way To GO
A Marketing Way To Go
A Missing Way To Go
A Showering Way To Go
Poison In The Candy Cane
Kendra Detective Mystery Collection Volume 1
Kendra Detective Mystery Collection Volume 2
Mystery Short Story Collection Volume 1
Mystery Short Story Collection Volume 2
Criminal Performance

Candy Detectives
Key To Birth In The Past

<u>Science Fiction Short Stories:</u>
Their Brave New World
Gummy Bear Detective
The Candy Detective
What Candies Fear
The Blurred Image
Shattered Legions
The First Rememberer
Life of A Rememberer
System of Wonder
Lifesaver
Remarkable Way She Died
The Interrogation of Annabella Stormic
Blade of The Emperor
Arbiter's Truth
Computation of Battle
Old One's Wrath
Puppets and Masters
Ship of Plague
Interrogation
Edge of Failure

<u>Fantasy Short Stories:</u>
City of Snow

MYSTERY SHORT STORY COLLECTION VOLUME 4

City of Light
City of Vengeance
Dragons, Goats and Kingdom
Smog The Pathetic Dragon
Don't Go In The Shed
The Tomato Saver
The Remarkable Way She Died
Dragon Coins
Dragon Tea
Dragon Rider

All books in 'An Introductory Series':
Clinical Psychology and Transgender Clients
Clinical Psychology
Careers In Psychology
Psychology of Suicide
Dementia Psychology
Clinical Psychology Reflections Volume 4
Forensic Psychology of Terrorism And Hostage-Taking
Forensic Psychology of False Allegations
Year In Psychology
CBT For Anxiety
CBT For Depression
Applied Psychology
BIOLOGICAL PSYCHOLOGY 3ʳᴰ EDITION

COGNITIVE PSYCHOLOGY THIRD EDITION
SOCIAL PSYCHOLOGY- 3RD EDITION
ABNORMAL PSYCHOLOGY 3RD EDITION
PSYCHOLOGY OF RELATIONSHIPS- 3RD EDITION
DEVELOPMENTAL PSYCHOLOGY 3RD EDITION
HEALTH PSYCHOLOGY
RESEARCH IN PSYCHOLOGY
A GUIDE TO MENTAL HEALTH AND TREATMENT AROUND THE WORLD- A GLOBAL LOOK AT DEPRESSION
FORENSIC PSYCHOLOGY
THE FORENSIC PSYCHOLOGY OF THEFT, BURGLARY AND OTHER CRIMES AGAINST PROPERTY
CRIMINAL PROFILING: A FORENSIC PSYCHOLOGY GUIDE TO FBI PROFILING AND GEOGRAPHICAL AND STATISTICAL PROFILING.
CLINICAL PSYCHOLOGY
FORMULATION IN PSYCHOTHERAPY
PERSONALITY PSYCHOLOGY AND INDIVIDUAL DIFFERENCES
CLINICAL PSYCHOLOGY

MYSTERY SHORT STORY COLLECTION VOLUME 4

REFLECTIONS VOLUME 1
CLINICAL PSYCHOLOGY
REFLECTIONS VOLUME 2
Clinical Psychology Reflections Volume 3
CULT PSYCHOLOGY
Police Psychology

A Psychology Student's Guide To University
How Does University Work?
A Student's Guide To University And Learning
University Mental Health and Mindset

www.ingramcontent.com/pod-product-compliance
Lightning Source LLC
LaVergne TN
LVHW011857060526
838200LV00054B/4389